W9-BFM-674

the CRITTER club

 ## Ellie Tames the Tiger

by Callie Barkley ♥ illustrated by Tracy Bishop

LITTLE SIMON
New York   London   Toronto   Sydney   New Delhi

LITTLE SIMON

An imprint of Simon & Schuster Children's Publishing Division · 1230 Avenue of the Americas, New York, New York 10020 · First Little Simon hardcover edition March 2021. Copyright © 2021 by Simon & Schuster, Inc. All rights reserved, including the right of reproduction in whole or in part in any form.

LITTLE SIMON is a registered trademark of Simon & Schuster, Inc., and associated colophon is a trademark of Simon & Schuster, Inc. For information about special discounts for bulk purchases, please contact Simon & Schuster Special Sales at 1-866-506-1949 or business@simonandschuster.com.

The Simon & Schuster Speakers Bureau can bring authors to your live event. For more information or to book an event contact the Simon & Schuster Speakers Bureau at 1-866-248-3049 or visit our website at www.simonspeakers.com.

Designed by Brittany Fetcho. The text of this book was set in ITC Stone Informal Std. Manufactured in the United States of America 0221 FFG. 10 9 8 7 6 5 4 3 2 1

Cataloging-in-Publication data for this title is available from the Library of Congress.

ISBN 978-1-5344-8065-0 (hc)

ISBN 978-1-5344-8064-3 (pbk)

ISBN 978-1-5344-8066-7 (eBook)

Table of Contents

One Wrong Move

It was Ellie Mitchell's favorite day of the week: Wednesday, which was drama club day at school. And this was an extra-special one. They were about to run a dress rehearsal for their play, *Amazing Animal Acts*. Ellie had been cast as Cat. She would be onstage in her costume for the very first time!

Ellie adored her costume. She and her mom had made it together. They started with an orange unitard. Then they added brown ruffles and furry trim.

But the best part was the long, springy cat tail. It bobbed and bounced when Ellie leaped and jumped.

My tail will really *help me get into character*, Ellie thought.

Inside the auditorium, Mrs. Jameson, the drama teacher, called all the actors over.

"Only one week until opening night," Mrs. Jameson said excitedly. "So we're going to run the whole show today. But first I want to make one change to Cat's big dance number."

Cat! That's me! thought Ellie.

"Ellie, I've added another cat dancer," said Mrs. Jameson.

Ellie's shoulders drooped. That number was her big moment in the play!

Mrs. Jameson explained what she had in mind. With two dancers, they could add a few partner moves. The dance would be a little bit longer. And there could be a big swing dance finish. It would make the dance *twice* as exciting.

Ellie smiled. She was willing to give it a try!

Mrs. Jameson said that Ellie's costar would be Paul, another second grader.

"We'll get you a cat costume, Paul," Mrs. Jameson said. "For now, let's run through the dance."

She showed Ellie and Paul the moves. They were swing dance steps: rock steps, triple steps, swingouts, and side-by-side moves. Mrs. Jameson demonstrated. Then Ellie and Paul gave it a try.

"Great!" Mrs. Jameson said. "Just one more."

The last move was called an underarm turn. Holding Ellie's hand, Paul lifted his arm. Ellie twirled underneath. Then Paul let go of her hand and Ellie spun away.

"Let's see that one more time," Mrs. Jameson said.

Paul lifted his arm. Ellie twirled underneath—once . . . twice . . . Then suddenly there was a loud *rip*!

"Oh no!" Ellie cried.

She turned to see the back of her unitard. Paul was stepping on her cat tail! Luckily, the tail was still attached, but only by a thread.

Ellie looked up at Paul. He took a step back.

"Aren't you going to apologize?" she asked impatiently.

"What do you mean?" Paul replied. "It was an accident."

Ellie knew that. But . . . her beautiful costume! Paul wasn't going to say he was sorry? She crossed her arms and stared at him.

Suddenly, Paul's face turned very red.

"I said I didn't mean to!" he cried. Then he ran off the stage and out of the auditorium without looking back.

Mrs. Jameson had said adding Paul would make the dance twice as exciting . . . not twice as hard!

Chapter 2

New Cat in Town

Ellie was still feeling annoyed at the end of rehearsal. But she was too rushed to do anything about it. She had to meet up with Liz, Amy, and Marion at the Critter Club. That was the animal rescue shelter the friends had started together.

They all loved animals, and

Amy's mom was a veterinarian. Plus their friend Ms. Sullivan had offered her barn as the location. So it was the perfect way for the girls to help the lost and lonely animals of Santa Vista.

Ellie's dad picked her up and they drove across town to the Critter Club. That week, the girls were pet sitting an aquarium full of tropical fish and a frog in a glass tank.

Marion, Liz, and Amy were already there. Marion had her clipboard out.

"Sorry," Ellie said, hurrying in. "I came straight from drama club."

"That's okay," Marion replied. "I think we figured out the schedule. We only put you down for Friday after school. Does that work?"

"We can handle the other days
since we know you have a lot going
on with the play," Amy added.

Liz clapped. "We're so excited to
come see it!" she exclaimed.

Ellie smiled. Her friends were the
best. "Thanks! I just hope we'll be
ready."

The girls gave her puzzled looks. "What do you mean?" Amy asked gently.

Ellie told them all about dress rehearsal. It was bad enough she now had to share her big dance. But on top of it, Paul seemed kind of clumsy. He had ripped her beautiful costume. "And he didn't even say he was sorry!" Ellie cried.

Amy frowned. "That's odd," she said. "The other day by the lockers, Paul accidentally bumped me as he walked by. I dropped my books. But he kept going." Amy shrugged. "He didn't even turn around—or help me pick them up."

"See? Rude!" Ellie declared.

"Hmm, I don't know," Marion said skeptically. "We don't know him very well. I mean, he only moved here a few months ago."

That's no excuse to be rude, Ellie was about to say.

But just then, Ms. Sullivan came in through the barn door. She was carrying a large cardboard box.

"Girls, you have another guest," Ms. Sullivan said excitedly.

Ellie heard a *mew* from inside the box. A cat?!

"A friend of mine found this stray," Ms. Sullivan went on. "But she already has a cat and she can't keep both."

The girls crowded around Ms. Sullivan. They leaned in to look.

Inside the box was an adorable kitten! His fur was a swirl of light brown with darker brown spots. And he had some stripes, too.

"Dr. Purvis already checked him out," Ms. Sullivan said. "He's a Bengal cat. And he's healthy. All he needs is a home."

"He is sooo beautiful," Marion said.

Liz added, "He looks just like a—"

"Tiger!" all four of them said together.

Ellie smiled at her friends. "That's the perfect name!" she said. "Tiger!"

Chapter 3

What Goes Up Must Come Down

Amy gently lifted Tiger out of the box. She put him down on the barn floor. He stood and blinked. Then he raised his nose and sniffed the air. But he stood frozen to the spot.

Marion sat down on the floor next to Tiger. She was good with cats. Marion had her own cat named

Ollie. And she once helped a shy cat named Tabby who had come to the Critter Club.

Right away, Tiger jumped into Marion's lap. He let her pet him. Soon Tiger was climbing up into Marion's arms. She wrapped her arms around him and stood up slowly. Tiger purred.

"You can tell he likes being held," Liz observed.

Marion slowly carried Tiger around the barn. "How about I introduce you to the other animals?" she asked Tiger.

Suddenly, Tiger leaped out of Marion's arms with a *yowl*! He darted away, a small blur of brown fur.

"Yowl!" Tiger cried again. He ran under a table and into a dark corner. Ellie followed, thinking she could block his way out. But Tiger was too fast! He darted to Ellie's left and sped past her.

In a flash, Tiger was up on top of the frog tank.

"Tiger, no!" Amy shouted as she took a step toward the cat.

Tiger leaped to the next table. He climbed onto the aquarium. "Look out!" Liz cried. "The top isn't closed!"

Tiger perched on the edge of the aquarium. He dipped a paw into the water, trying to scoop out a fish. Then, for a moment, he stood frozen, watching the fish swim.

He's distracted, thought Ellie. She snuck up behind Tiger. But before she could grab him, Tiger leaped away! He was off and racing around the barn again.

Ellie sighed in frustration. She'd been so close!

Tiger jumped onto one hay bale, then another. Then he jumped onto an even taller stack of hay bales. He went higher and higher. In seconds, he was perched on one of the beams in the ceiling.

Then Tiger stopped. He couldn't go any higher. He looked around as if unsure where to go next.

The girls looked at one another. "What do we do now?" Ellie asked.

"I don't know," said Liz. "We can't follow him up there. Maybe we just wait?"

"He has to come down, right?" said Marion. "When he gets hungry?"

Amy nodded, then stopped. "Unless he can't," she said. "Unless he's stuck!"

chapter 4

Rescue That Tiger!

Amy hurried off to find Ms. Sullivan. Meanwhile, Ellie, Liz, and Marion tried to get Tiger to come down.

Ellie called to him in a high-pitched voice. "Here, Tiger! Here, kitty kitty!"

Tiger looked at her. But he didn't climb down.

37

Liz shook a toy mouse that she found inside Tiger's box. "Come on, Tiger!" she called out. "Come down and play." But Tiger didn't budge.

Marion pulled a bag of cat food out of a storage cabinet. She poured some into a pet food dish. "Tiger!" Marion said. "Time for food!"

Nothing worked.

Amy came back with Ms. Sullivan right behind her. Now Tiger was up in the rafters!

Ms. Sullivan frowned. "I see what you mean," she said. "He *is* up very high."

Then as they all watched, Tiger
stood up on the beam. He started
pacing back and forth.

"Careful, Tiger!" Ellie called out.

The cat made a move to jump
down onto the highest hay bale.
But he stopped himself. "Yowl!"
Tiger cried out.

Ms. Sullivan turned to the girls. "I'm worried he'll hurt himself," she told them. "I think we'd better call the fire department." She hurried to the house.

Within five minutes, a fire truck pulled up in Ms. Sullivan's driveway.

Three firefighters carried a big ladder into the barn. They extended it high enough to reach Tiger. Two firefighters held it steady while the third started climbing.

As she got close to Tiger, Ellie held her breath. What if he darted away?

But when the firefighter reached out, Tiger climbed into her arms.

In seconds, they were both back on the ground, safe and sound.

The girls crowded around to thank the firefighters.

"Happy to help," one of them said. "Let's unstack these hay bales so he can't climb up again."

Ms. Sullivan decided to take Tiger to Dr. Purvis for a quick check-up. "Just to make sure he's okay," she told them. "Why don't you girls head home?"

Part of Ellie wanted to go with Ms. Sullivan and Tiger. But another part was happy to go home. Between rehearsal and Tiger, it had been a long day. Ellie was tired.

After dinner and homework, Ellie flopped into bed. Before she knew it, she was sound asleep.

chapter 5

The Class Project

Ellie was onstage, dancing in the spotlight. Her springy cat tail bobbed as she leaped perfectly in time to the music.

Ellie turned her head. There was Tiger, dancing at her side. Amazingly, he knew all the dance steps! Rock step, triple step, triple step . . .

In slow motion, a carpet-covered climbing tower descended from above. Tiger danced over to it and jumped up onto the first level. Ellie did too. She was so light on her feet!

Together they jumped up to the next level . . . and the next. They were almost as high as the colored stage lights.

Just then, Ellie felt a hand on her shoulder.

She opened her eyes. Morning
light peeked in around her bedroom
curtains. Her mom was standing
over her bed. "Ellie? Wake-up time,"
Mrs. Mitchell said gently. "You were
meowing in your sleep."

Ellie rubbed her eyes and laughed. "Just a funny dream. A *very* funny dream."

Ellie had overslept a little bit. She rushed to get ready and hurried off to school.

In the classroom, Ellie spotted Liz. Ellie headed toward her, knowing Liz would laugh about the cat dream.

But their teacher, Mrs. Sienna, was already asking for their attention. Ellie plopped into her seat.

"Class," Mrs. Sienna said, "we're starting our geography project today."

Each student would be paired up with a partner. Mrs. Sienna would assign them a country to research. Then they would make an informational poster.

"Please pay attention while I read off the pairs," Mrs. Sienna said.

Amy was paired with a classmate, then Liz's partner was assigned. Ellie sighed. Was it too much to hope she'd be partnered up with Marion?

Finally, she heard her name. "Ellie," Mrs. Sienna said, "and Paul. Your country is Brazil."

Wait. Paul? First play rehearsals and now this project, too? Ugh. They'd already had one problem.

Then again, they *did* have to learn to work together.

Ellie decided to give Paul another chance.

Later, on the way to lunch, Ellie caught up to Paul in the hallway.

"Paul, hi!" she said. "So, Brazil? What do you think is the best way to start?"

Paul looked startled. He didn't answer right away. So Ellie went on.

"I think we could take notes on index cards first," she suggested. "Then next week we could start the poster."

Paul opened his mouth to reply. But Ellie wasn't done.

"I mean, that's how we did it for my last partner project," Ellie said. "It worked out great!"

Paul frowned.

Ellie shrugged. "I think it's probably the best plan," she added.

She paused. This time, she waited through five long seconds of silence.

"So what do you think?" Ellie asked.

Paul stopped walking and turned to face Ellie. "Whatever you say!" Paul blurted out. "You're the boss!"

Paul hurried away down the hall. Ellie stood staring after him.

She was so confused. She was just trying to be nice. But Paul wasn't making it easy!

Out of Step

On Friday at lunchtime, Mrs. Jameson came to find Ellie. She was at a table with Liz, Amy, and Marion. The teachers were about to ring the bell for recess.

"There you are, Ellie!" Mrs. Jameson said brightly. "Feel like some dance practice during recess?"

"Oh, sure!" Ellie replied. "I could run through my steps with you."

"Actually," said Mrs. Jameson, "I meant you and *Paul* could practice." Mrs. Jameson stepped to one side. Paul was right behind her.

Ellie bit her lip. "Oh," she said
hesitantly. She glanced at Paul. He
didn't look happy about it either.

In fact, he looked very unhappy.
Ellie felt bad for him.

Ellie took a deep breath. "Sure!"
she said, trying to sound cheerful.
"Why not?"

Mrs. Jameson gave a thumbs-up. "Great! You two can use the stage." She led the way to the auditorium. Paul followed her.

Ellie quickly gathered up her things. "Wish me luck," she whispered to her friends as she rushed away.

Liz, Marion, and Amy smiled encouragingly. "You've got this," Liz said. Ellie wasn't so sure.

On stage, Mrs. Jameson reviewed the dance steps for Ellie and Paul. Then she suggested they practice on their own.

"I'll be next door if you need me," Mrs. Jameson told them. She went out through the stage-left door.

When it closed, the sound echoed through the big auditorium. Ellie and Paul were alone.

"Well," said Ellie, "want to give it a try?"

Paul shrugged. "Might as well."

So they began. They were fine through the side-by-side moves.

They were a tiny bit out of sync on the triple steps, but nothing terrible.

Then they got to the first swingout. Paul let go of Ellie's hand and they lost the beat.

"Let's just start again," Ellie suggested.

This time, they were totally together until the underarm turn. Paul forgot to lift his arm up. Ellie spun right into it.

"Oof!" she said.

Paul sighed in frustration.

They tried it a third time. The triple steps were perfect. They nailed the swingouts. Halfway through, Ellie smiled. *We're getting it,* she thought.

Then Paul tripped on the last rock step. His foot came down on Ellie's toe. It didn't hurt, but Ellie stopped dancing.

"That was so much better!" Ellie said hopefully. "But maybe we should stop for today?"

Paul nodded.

Ellie went to grab her lunch bag at the foot of the stage. "New routines take time to learn," Ellie said. Then she turned back toward Paul.

He was already walking out the auditorium door.

"Hey, wait!" Ellie called. "Paul?"
She hurried after him. Was he upset?

By the time she got to the door, Paul was halfway down the hall. He greeted two friends coming in from recess. Ellie saw Paul say something to them. They all looked back at Ellie. Then they all walked off down the hall.

What had Paul said to them?

Ellie had a feeling it wasn't very nice.

The Great Escape

At least Ellie had Tiger to look forward to. It was Friday—her day at the Critter Club after school. Marion was also on the schedule. She was already in the barn when Ellie arrived.

And she looked panicked.

"What's the matter?" Ellie asked.

Marion pointed at one of the pet crates.

"Amy's mom suggested we keep Tiger in the crate," Marion said. "Just when no one is around. But when I got here, the door was open."

Ellie looked more closely. The crate was empty! Where was Tiger?

Right away, Ellie looked up at the ceiling. Phew! He wasn't up on a beam again.

Ellie and Marion searched the barn. They didn't see Tiger anywhere.

But then Marion grabbed Ellie's arm. "Shh," she said. "Hear that?"

Ellie listened. *Rustle, rustle.* What *was* that? It was coming from the wall of cabinets.

The girls tiptoed over. They followed the sound to a bottom cabinet. The cabinet door was slightly ajar. Ellie swung the door open.

There was Tiger! His head was inside a giant bag of dry cat food.

"Tiger!" Marion cried.

Tiger pulled his head out and looked up at Ellie and Marion. Then he ducked back into the bag for more food. *Rustle, rustle.*

"Come out of there," Ellie said. "You'll get sick from eating so much!"

Tiger was so distracted that it was easy for Ellie to scoop him up. She carried him back to the crate and put him inside.

"How did he get out?" Marion wondered. "Maybe Liz or Amy didn't latch the door yesterday?"

Ellie shrugged. "But then how did he open the cabinet?" she replied. Ellie sat down on a hay bale to think. "So he's fast. He's a climber. *And* he can open doors?"

Out of the corner of her eye, Ellie saw movement inside the crate. She turned.

"Look!" Ellie said with a gasp.

Tiger was batting at the door latch. With each tap, the latch slid over a tiny bit. Bit by bit, Tiger was unlocking it.

Marion grabbed a dog leash off a wall hook. Then she hurried over to the crate. She clipped the leash into a hole by the latch handle. It blocked the latch from sliding.

Marion and Ellie looked at each other with wide eyes.

"This cat is full of surprises!" Marion exclaimed.

"Maybe it's time to learn more about Tiger," Ellie said. "Before there are even *more* surprises!"

Chapter 8

A Cat Expert

On Saturday morning, Ellie went along with her Nana Gloria to the Santa Vista Library.

While Nana Gloria checked out the audiobooks, Ellie headed to the children's department. She was on the hunt for books about cats.

Ellie quickly found the nonfiction

section on animals. She flipped through books on caring for a new kitten. She found books about different cat breeds. Some even had info on Bengals. But they didn't say much about behavior.

So Ellie sat down at one of the library computers. She searched "Bengal behavior" and began to read.

A few adjectives caught Ellie's eye. They were *active, curious,* and *highly intelligent.*

"I'll say," Ellie said out loud.

"You'll say what?" said a voice behind her.

Ellie turned. It was Paul! He was sitting at a computer in the next row.

"Oh, hi," she said. She wasn't sure what else to say. Ellie turned back to her computer screen. Then curiosity got the best of her. She turned around again. "What are you doing here?" Ellie asked.

"Research," Paul replied. "On Brazil."

Rude, thought Ellie. *Starting the project without me!*

"You like cats?" Paul asked.

Ellie eyed him suspiciously. "How did you—?" Then she realized that from where he was sitting, Paul could see Ellie's screen. "Oh. Yes. I mean, I don't have any. But I'm helping take care of one."

97

"A Bengal?" Paul asked, pointing to her screen. "Those are great cats. My best friend from my old hometown has one. They need to play a lot, though. They have so much energy! They need room to climb. And did you know they like water?"

Ellie looked at Paul in awe.

First of all, this was the most Ellie had heard Paul talk—ever. Who knew he liked cats so much?

Second, he was describing Tiger exactly! Tiger leaping around the Critter Club barn. Tiger climbing onto a high beam. Tiger going fishing in the aquarium.

Paul came to sit down at the computer next to Ellie's. He pointed at the website she was reading.

"I didn't know this, though," Paul said. He read out loud: "'If a Bengal is bored, she might make games for herself like opening drawers or taking things apart.'" Paul looked at Ellie. "They can open things?"

"Yes!" Ellie replied. She told Paul about how Tiger had gotten out of his crate at the Critter Club. "I'm worried. How do we keep him safe until he's adopted?" Ellie said. "And if he's so much trouble, will anyone *want* to adopt him?"

Paul was quiet for a bit. Then he said, "Well, does he seem happy? Cats can talk to us in all kinds of ways. Tilting their ears back. How they hold their tail. Stuff like that." Paul looked down. His voice got quieter. "He is in a brand-new place. It can be hard. Especially when everything around you is new and different."

Ellie looked at Paul. Wait. Was he talking about Tiger? Or was he talking about . . . himself?

A light bulb went on in Ellie's mind.

❧ CAT LANGUAGE ❧

INTERESTED

FRIENDLY

RELAXED

SCARED

ANNOYED

Two of a Kind

Ellie invited Paul to come meet Tiger the next day. She was a little surprised when he said yes. But she was glad, too.

Ellie realized she'd been wrong about Paul. He wasn't rude. He was still getting used to his new school—just like Tiger was getting used to the Critter Club. They were both a little nervous.

"This is perfect," Ellie told Paul when he got to the barn on Sunday. "You know so much about cats. Maybe you can tell how Tiger is feeling."

"I'll do my best," Paul replied. He held up a tote bag. "I brought a bunch of cat toys. We can see if Tiger likes any of them."

Ellie brought him over to Tiger's cat crate. They let the cat out and sat down on the floor, ready to play. But Tiger bolted away from them.

"Tiger, come back!" Ellie called. She made a move to chase him. But Paul stopped her.

"Let him run a little bit," he said. "Maybe he just needs to get his energy out."

So Ellie and Paul sat and waited. Meanwhile, Tiger ran laps around the barn.

In a bit, Paul pulled out a toy—a felt fish on a string tied to the end of a stick. "Let's see if Tiger likes this."

Paul held the stick so the fish just barely touched the floor. Then he shook it. The fish wiggled and flopped.

Like a bolt of lightning, Tiger came racing over. He tried to pounce on the fish. At the last moment, Paul yanked it away. Tiger missed and bumped gently into a table leg. He pounced again. Paul yanked it away four or five times. Then he let Tiger catch it.

"Whoa!" Ellie cried. "He likes it!"

Paul nodded. "I think all Tiger needs is to play," Paul said. "He's just a high energy cat. And maybe a little clumsy," he said with a laugh.

Then Paul was quiet for a moment.

"I know I can be a little clumsy, too," he went on. "You know, like with the dancing. It's embarrassing. I—I was too embarrassed to say sorry." He looked up at her. "So . . . sorry."

Ellie smiled. *That makes sense,*

she thought. And that story Amy had told—how Paul had bumped into her? Ellie felt sure that was an accident too.

"I understand," Ellie told Paul.

There was just one thing that was still bothering her. Ellie asked Paul about Friday—when he'd said something to his friends. "Was it about me?" she asked.

Paul nodded. "I told them I wish I could dance as well as you," he said.

Aww, thought Ellie.

She watched as Tiger climbed into Paul's lap. Tiger nudged at Paul's hand with his nose. He kept doing it until Paul pet him. Then Tiger purred loudly.

"You know," Paul said, "our house has a lot of room. Like, for a climbing tower. And my mom works from home. She could play with Tiger during the day. And then I could play with him after school. Do you think, if my mom says yes, I could adopt him?"

Ellie gasped. Of course! Tiger and Paul were meant for each other!

Chapter 10

Cat Dancers

Opening night was finally here! Ellie peeked out into the audience from backstage. *Gosh, there are a lot of people.*

Next to her, Paul put on his cat ears. "Do you see your family?" he asked.

Ellie nodded. She saw her mom,

dad, her brother Toby, and Nana Gloria. Then she noticed Marion, Liz, and Amy. They were all there to see her perform!

"I'm nervous," she told Paul. It was the first time they would be dancing together in front of a real, live audience.

"Don't worry," Paul told her. "We've practiced so much."

He was right. They'd had five more rehearsals.

"Now you're more confident than I am!" Ellie said.

Paul nodded. "I know we can do it," he said. "Just remember: high energy! Like Tiger."

"If Tiger could swing dance," Ellie added with a laugh. But Paul was right.

We slink, we leap, we pounce. We are cat dancers, thought Ellie.

When their big number came, Ellie jumped out onto the stage with a spring in her step. Paul was right beside her.

Their cat dance went perfectly. Ellie knew Paul would tell Tiger all about it once he brought the cat home.

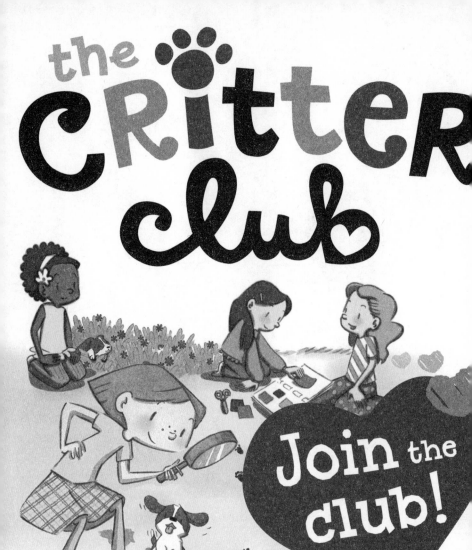

the CRITTER club

Join the club!